Thomas P. Lewis

The Blue Rocket Fun Show
or, Friends Forever!

Pictures by Ib Ohlsson

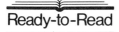

Ready-to-Read

Macmillan Publishing Company
New York
Collier Macmillan Publishers
London

Text copyright © 1986 by Thomas P. Lewis
Illustrations copyright © 1986 by Ib Ohlsson
Macmillan Publishing Company
866 Third Avenue, New York, N.Y. 10022
Collier Macmillan Canada, Inc.
Printed in the United States of America
10   9   8   7   6   5   4   3   2   1

The text of this book is set in 18 pt. Century Expanded.
The illustrations are preseparated, rendered in ink and pencil,
and reproduced in three colors.

Library of Congress Cataloging-in-Publication Data

Lewis, Thomas P.
The blue rocket fun show, or, Friends forever!
(Ready-to-read)
Summary: Leslie loves to visit the carnival where
her new best friend, Niki, lives, but it isn't until
the carnival is ready to leave town that she learns
the secret of Niki's real home.
[1. Friendship – Fiction. 2. Amusement parks –
Fiction. 3. Science fiction] I. Ohlsson, Ib,
date, ill. II. Title. III. Title: Friends
forever! IV. Series.
PZ7.L5882Bl   1986   [E]   85-13631
ISBN 0-02-758810-6

For Lauren Wohl
– T. P. L.

For Ria
– I. O.

Leslie and Niki
were new best friends.
Niki had come to the city,
just for the summer,
with the Blue Rocket Fun Show.

She lived in the park
in a bug-like house,
next to all the animals
and the rides.

Leslie and Niki
did everything together.
They both liked movies and books
about rocket ships and stars
and faraway planets up in the sky.
They saw movies like *Star Wars*,
Supergirl and *E.T.*
over and over again.

7

At night, when there were no clouds,
they went to the roof
of Leslie's apartment building.
Leslie brought her telescope.

Up close, the moon looked like
the skin of a silver orange.
"The dark parts are called seas,"
Niki said. "But
there is no water in them."
They found the Big Dipper,
which looked like a cooking pan
floating through the sky.
The Big Dipper was made of
seven stars.

It seemed to point to another star.
"That is Polaris, the North Star,"
Niki said.
"It is really *three* stars.
They are so close together
they look like one."

Niki and Leslie had sleep-overs
almost every night.
Sometimes they slept at Leslie's,
and sometimes they slept at Niki's.
Niki did not sleep on a regular bed.
She slept on pillows
inside a jar-like thing.

There was plenty of room there
for Leslie, too,
and their dolls and stuffed animals.
Part of the jar was a screen.
They could watch TV shows
inside the jar.

"I hope we stay friends *forever*,"
Leslie said.

"Me, too," Niki said.

Niki's mother heard them talking.
"What, you girls still up?
Lights out, you two," she said.
But, first, she gave them
a good-night treat.
"What is this?" Leslie asked.
"It is called *zer-glop*,"
Niki said. "Isn't it delicious?
Would you like some more?"

"No, thank you," Leslie said.

It was very strange.

She thought it tasted like

vanilla toothpaste.

But she did not say so.

Leslie and Niki

did many things together in the city.

They swam in a pool

and made a house inside a statue.

But the most fun of all
was at the Blue Rocket Fun Show.
They rode the Flashing Comet
Bumper Cars six times in a row.

They rode animals with two heads
and three eyes
on the Outer-Space Merry-Go-Round.
"It is like being
on a different world," Leslie said.

Sometimes Leslie's brother Paul
came with them.
They rode in space suits
that floated in balloons.

Leslie and Niki
showed Paul a metal hut
filled with wheels and levers
and computer screens.
"All of the Fun Show
is run from here," Leslie said.

20

"The Loop-the-Loop Racer,
the Gyro Twist,
the Space Caterpillar—everything."
"Watch, now," said a man
with funny pointed ears.
"This starts the Big Wheel.
You can see it turn on this screen."
"Totally awesome!" said Paul.

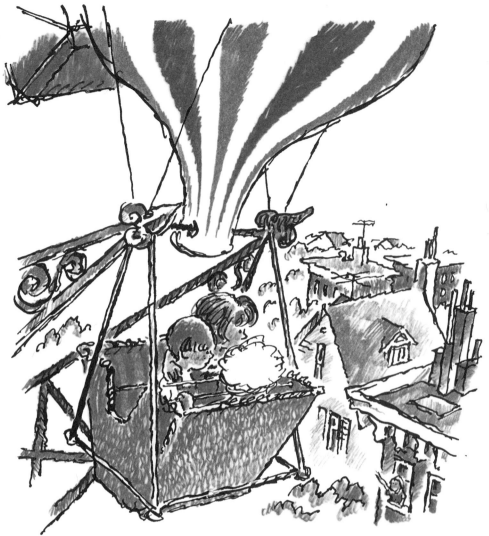

After that, Niki's mother gave them
an extra-long ride on the Big Wheel.
From the top they could see
Leslie and Paul's mother,
waving from her window.

When they came down, Niki's father
gave them *plunk-whip* on a stick.
"Phew!" said Paul.
"This tastes like day-old cereal
covered with rotten tomatoes!"
"Shh, Paul—that isn't nice,"
said Leslie.
But she did not like it, either!

"Niki," said Niki's father,
"why don't you take your friends
  for a ride on Sofi?"
"Is that Sofi?" asked Paul.
"Yes," said Niki.
"That is Aunt Sofi....
  I mean, yes, it is."
Sofi kneeled down.

She gave Paul a push up
with her funny trunk.
Then she helped Leslie and Niki up
with her tail.
"Elephants are bigger
than I thought," Paul said.
"Sofi is not an elephant,"
said Niki.

They rocked from side to side.

"Careful, children.

Duck your heads."

"Who said that?" said Paul.

"I didn't," said Leslie.

Niki laughed.

"It must have been the wind!"

At the end of the ride,
Sofi kneeled again.
She put her head down
so that they could slide off.
"Thank you," Leslie said.
"You are welcome, I am sure."
"There it goes again,"
said Paul. "The wind!"

It was the best summer
Leslie had ever had.
She and Niki
read storybooks together
on the roof of Leslie's house.

They took each other's picture.

Sometimes, Leslie brought
her china animals
to a hill near the Fun Show.

There, the two friends
played in the grass
with her four cats, dog, owl,
penguin, panda, brown bear,
giraffe, three horses, panther,
elephant, lion, tiger, skunk
and raccoon.

Only one thing made Leslie sad.

"When will you go away, Niki?"
she asked.

"Soon," said Niki.

"I will miss you," Leslie said.

"I will miss you, too."

"I want to write to you,"
Leslie said. "But I don't know
where you live."
"I...I...it is very far away,"
Niki said.

One day Niki said,

"I am not supposed to tell.

But you are my best friend.

We are going away tonight."

"Oh!" said Leslie.

"Leslie, there is something else
I want to tell you.
But it is very hard.
I...I don't want you
to be afraid of me."
"Best friends aren't afraid
when they are together,"
Leslie said.
"I am not like you," Niki said.
"I am not a human.

"We come from the sky.
We are called Fludgelings.
Our home is on the planet Fludge."
"Niki!" Leslie said.
"That is wonderful!"

"You cannot see Fludge," Niki said.
"But you can find where we are.
In September,
go outside at night.
We will be on the other side of
Polaris, the North Star.
Our planet has a sun like yours.
It keeps us warm
and gives us light."

37

"May I come to say good-bye
tonight?" asked Leslie.

"I hoped you would," Niki said.

"Paul can come, too, if you'd like."

That night Leslie and Paul
rode all the rides for the last time.

38

They played a last game
of Toss-the-Donut. Leslie won
a stuffed blue and yellow myna bird.
At last the rides stopped.
People left the Blue Rocket
Fun Show and went home.
Gates were locked.

"It is time for Leslie and Paul
to go, too," Niki's mother said.
"Please let them stay, Mama,"
Niki said. "They are my friends."

Niki's mother said,
"Leslie, are you a brave girl?
Will you try not to be afraid
even if you see something
very, very strange?"

"I...I will try," Leslie said.

"Paul, can you be brave, too?"

"Yes," said Paul.

"Very well. You both may stay."

Niki's father clapped his hands.
Then many strange,
wonderful things happened.
The Loop-the-Loop Racer
began to move.

It joined the Gyro Twist.

The Big Wheel slid over on top.

All the other rides came together

to make a single blue spaceship.

Then Niki began to change.
"Don't be afraid, Leslie,"
she said.
Her nose grew long.
Her ears went away.
She looked very different,
but Leslie could see
that she was still Niki.

All the others changed, too.

Aunt Sofi's trunk grew shorter.

Her ears became pointed.

Niki's mother grew a tail.

Her father's neck grew long.

"It is time to say good-bye,"
  Niki said.

"I have brought you
  two presents, Niki," Leslie said.

"The first is a box
  of inch-thick chocolate bars.
  I hope they won't melt,
  up there on Fludge.

"The other is a locket.
It has my picture in it.
I have one, too,
with your picture in it."
"We will be best friends—
forever!" Niki said.
Leslie and Niki hugged each other.
Niki hugged Paul, too.

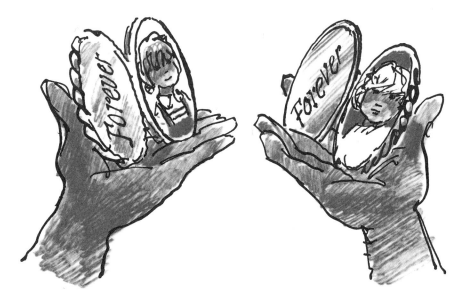

Then Niki went inside the spaceship
with her mother, her father
and all the other Fludgelings.

The door was shut.

Leslie cried while Paul waved.

She could not help it.

Many weeks passed. School began.
Oak leaves and maple leaves
began to fall in the park.
Paul and Leslie liked to walk there
and climb the rocks.
They sailed Paul's boat
across the pond.

One day, after school,

Leslie and Paul found an envelope

on a plate in the hall.

It had no stamp on it.

It glowed with a blue light.

It said "To Leslie (and Paul)."

Paul picked it up.

"It is cold," he said.

He read the letter out loud.

"Dear Friends," the letter said.
"We have come home at last.
I miss you both, very much.
I wish you could visit.

"But, Leslie, I have your locket,
and I think of you always.
Please write to me.
You may use the same envelope
this letter came in.
Just put it back on the plate.
It will come to me.
Well, it is Porco 32 now,
and time to go to bed.
Love, Niki.

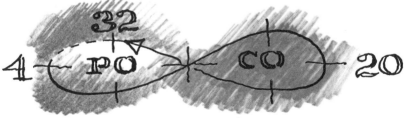

P.S.—I ate an inch-thick
chocolate bar today.
It was delicious!
There are only eleven left."

Paul shook his head.

"What do you think of that?"
he said.

Leslie said, "I think that,
someday,
I would like to see
the other side of the North Star."

She looked out her window,
past the trees and the birds—
past the clouds—
into the sky,
where, far away, Niki lived.